P9-DDL-323

TIGGY TIGER
Brave Explorer

To my brother, Paul
CF

To Susanna,
my sister and best friend
CJ

E
FRE

First published in Great Britain in 2001 by Orchard Books.
Text © Copyright 2001 by Claire Freedman.
Illustrations © Copyright 2001 by Cecilia Johansson.
First edition for the United States and Canada published in 2002 by Barron's Educational Series, Inc.

All inquiries should be addressed to:
Barron's Educational Series, Inc.
250 Wireless Boulevard
Hauppauge, NY 11788
http://www.barronseduc.com

International Standard Book Number 0-7641-2036-0
Library of Congress Catalog Card Number 2001089446

Printed in UAE
9 8 7 6 5 4 3 2 1

TIGGY TIGER
Brave Explorer

STORY BY
Claire Freedman

PICTURES BY
Cecilia Johansson

BARRON'S

The sun shone brightly above the banana trees. Another day had begun in the jungle.

"What do you want to do today?" Mom Tiger asked Tiggy.

"I want to be a brave explorer prowling through the jungle," Tiggy replied.

"Hello, Tiggy," said Hurly Monkey. "What game are you playing today?"

Tiggy said:

I am a brave explorer
Watch me leap and pounce and prowl

I want to be a roarer
So I'm practicing my growl!

Grrrr!

"When I'm a brave explorer,"
Hurly Monkey replied, "I love to
swing high up in the trees – like this!"
Tiggy watched him from below.
The trees looked very tall to him,
and he didn't feel quite brave
enough to join in.

"Aren't you scared you might fall?"
Tiggy called out.

"Oh no!" his friend cried back. "And
I know that if I did slip, my mom
would quickly catch me."

And Hurly Monkey sailed away, swinging
and swaying from branch to branch.

Tiggy pounced and bounced down to the river.
"Hello, Tiggy," said Tumble Turtle.
"What game are you playing today?"
Tiggy said:

I am a brave explorer
Watch me leap and pounce and prowl
Already I'm a roarer
With my little tiger growl!
Grrrrr!

splash!

"When I'm a brave explorer," Tumble Turtle replied, "I enjoy swimming across the river – like this!"

And with a splish and a splash Tumble Turtle dived in.

Tiggy watched from the shore. He dipped in his paw but the water looked very deep to him, and he didn't feel quite brave enough to join in.

"Aren't you scared you
might sink?" Tiggy shouted out.

"No chance!" his friend yelled back.
"Besides, if I did go under, my mom
would quickly scoop me up."

And he paddled away, while Tiggy
bounded further up the river bank.

"Hello, Tiggy," said Muddy Hippo.
"What game are you playing today?"

Tiggy said:

I am a brave explorer

Watch me leap and pounce and prowl

I am a mighty roarer

With my noisy tiger growl!

Grrrrrr!

"When I'm a brave explorer,"
Muddy Hippo replied, "I like to wallow
in the squishy, muddy swamp – like this!"
   Muddy Hippo squelched in the
soft oozy mud.

Squelch!

Tiggy skipped over to the bank. He put his nose toward the mud but the swamp seemed so boggy to him, and he didn't feel quite brave enough to join in.

"Aren't you scared you might get stuck?" he shouted out.

"Never!" his friend called back. "Anyway, if I did get stuck, my mom would quickly tug me free."

And Muddy Hippo went rolling and lolling in the sludgy swamp.

Suddenly...

The ground shook and the jungle rumbled.
CLUMP! THUMP! BUMPITY - BUMP!

"It's Mr. Grumpy Thumpy Rhinoceros!"
all the animals cried. "He's in a big
bad mood and he's coming this way!"

Everyone ran away – everyone except Tiggy.
He was far too busy having fun, pouncing and
bouncing, bounding and leaping on the shadows.

"Run, Tiggy, run!" his friends called to him. "Aren't you scared of Mr. Grumpy Thumpy Rhinoceros?"

"Not me!" Tiggy replied. "I'll simply growl and frighten him away!

Grrrrrrr!"

"But Tiggy," said Muddy Hippo, "What if your growl isn't loud enough?"

"I'm still not scared," said Tiggy, the brave explorer. "Because I know that even if my growl isn't big enough…

my mom's is!"

GRRRRRR!

And...

...Mr. Grumpy Thumpy Rhinoceros rumbled away!

Clump!

Thump!

Bumpity -
Bump !